LAKE OF EARTH

RUNNER-UP

2012 CAKETRAIN CHAPBOOK COMPETITION

MICHAEL KIMBALL, FINAL JUDGE

LAKE OF EARTH

WILLIAM VANDENBERG

CAKETRAIN
[a journal and press]

CAKETRAIN
[a journal and press]

Box 82588, Pittsburgh, Pennsylvania 15218

www.caketrain.org

Printed in the United States of America.

ISBN 978-0-9888915-3-1

TREATMENT

THIS ISN'T WORKING, he says. We doubt your commitment to the program.

I am not sure what he refers to. I am sitting in a wooden chair. We are both in a basement. I see feet shuffle past the high, narrow window.

I tell him that I don't understand. My body feels parched and cracked. Something has occurred that pulled me apart, and I am not sure I have been reassembled correctly.

You will sit here and keep an eye on the bench outside, he says.

I see three people sitting on the bench. I ask him what is going on.

Listen, he says. You will inform us when the situation changes.

I hear footsteps above us, the variable drone of music. I ask the man if he knows who lives upstairs and what is making all that noise.

It's not important. Watch the people on the bench.

I look up and out the window. The first occupant is stuffed in a leather jacket. He slouches—I see the dome of his shaved head rising over his shoulders. The second is a woman, I think, older, in a camelhair coat.

At some point the man exits, and I inhabit the basement by myself.

The third I can't be certain of. At first it was an old man in a black jacket, but now it is an obese woman. I search for an exit, but find none. Something changed! I yell. I bang my chair against the ceiling, but the noise from upstairs has ceased.

I sleep on the cold floor. Days pass. The new three do not change.

There were fixtures in the room once: a boiler, a rack of cleansers and rags, a bucket. They are gone now; only the window and the bare room remain.

And I notice how bright the sliver of sky has become.

The next day the people on the bench are erased by it.

Then the bench goes.

All that remains is a rectangle of light. The room is only a border. Then the room is gone.

Something has changed, I say. When the sound leaves me, I am unsure of where it comes from, where it goes.

Then I hear, Good, you are making progress.

FIVE CITIES

I

WE ARRIVED driving borrowed cars and you sewed a shirt wrong—you sewed the sleeve shut. I chipped the dishes you brought and we sometimes didn't eat or ate peanut butter from the jar and you cut off all your hair and tried to cut mine the same. I went barefoot until winter and during winter you hauled food home from the store and wore a thick wool coat. The floorboards creaked beneath us, with us. We worked at stands and kiosks and sold some of what we had accumulated. We slept the last night on the floor under a ceiling fan and sold the rest of it in the spirit of leaving.

WE ARRIVED in a city people vacated on weekends and you swapped out your button-downs for t-shirts and cutoffs. I exhibited my maturity by cleaning with bleach. We ate at a corner diner that never stopped calling us *hon* and you grew your hair back and vowed never to cut it again. You bought boots. We drove out of town to a giant grocery store that was bound to the highway and we gaped at it, in it. We spent a week at your uncle's cabin playing made-up dice games and swimming naked in the violet lake. I didn't have to work until your office figured you out and fired you and we got notices in the mail and on the door and we dreamed of bigger, more useful cities. In the morning we wrote out our curses in black marker on the walls and left.

WE ARRIVED on the coattails of an inheritance that cleared our debts and allowed us to buy a small box of space to claim as ours. I wore a belt that jangled all the time and you repaired the chipped hardwood floor with a glue gun. We ate in a nook. I put your hair in my mouth as a sign of respect and we wore sandals all the time because that's the kind of town it was. We kept bowls of candy and discovered a soft spot on the back of my neck that just buzzed. We vacationed in other cities and grew jealous of them and didn't work and stayed in all day. We called it *cultivation*. We developed a new technique involving wrists (we wrote the book on wrists). The money grew thin so we sold our new debt and I said one morning that I thought we were done. You took this to mean that it was time for us to pack up our things and leave again and I realized my mistake and declined to correct you.

4

WE ARRIVED at night before our belongings did. I buttoned my shirt as high as it would go and tried to button yours the same. You bought brushes and steel scrapers and they stole our food on the way back from the grocery store. You came home one day and wordlessly removed all your hair. They again stole our food coming back from the grocery store, this time with knives, and I didn't want to for a long time until I did. We saw your week in jail as a mandated vacation and no one would hire you so I worked all the time and you slept and slept and in your sleep told me about better cities, cities with homes and familiar people in them. We left attempting to prove you wrong.

I GREW TO LOVE the curve of your thumb. We never threw anything away and had takeout all the damn time. We wore the same hairstyle and people couldn't tell us apart and we bought thin, painful shoes. We never shopped at legit grocery stores, just ones labeled *convenience* with an unhealthy smear of products. The act, on its occasion, couldn't be described as you taking me or me taking you—we took each other and we took no vacations and we had no jobs and no money. The last city grew like a cave. We slept the last night in a locked, disgendered bathroom and I do not remember who left first and I do not remember if we left together and I do not remember if we left alone.

WIFE OF ELIJAH

HE SOMETIMES VIEWED the wife as a curse. He was prone
to sleeping rages. The wife watched air burst from his nostrils
at night. She would put her hand under his nose and feel the
warmth escape from him. They slept naked and sweated directly
into the sheets.

Their children grew, and he regarded them as ungainly. He got
two skinny girls with bulbous knees. The wife kept the memory of
how they smelled at different ages.

In the morning they made the girls ready for school, he the
younger, she the older. The parents whispered different things in
their ears, things the girls never told each other.

He planned on a third child but balked at the cost. The wife wanted a piano, and that was fine. They imagined the house filled with music. Instead the younger girl punctured their Sunday afternoons with idle plinks.

The older girl grew older and left. The younger girl regressed and had to be sent away. Her last act in the house involved a baking sheet and a pair of blackened hands. The parents visited her once a month and drank orange liquid together in the cafeteria.

The older girl came back and left again. Sometime after that the husband and wife had a good month, a really good month. He sat at the kitchen table and she stood next to him. She would pull his head to her stomach, smash his face in it a little, run her hands through his hair. She did this several times a week for the duration of the month. He kept a tally until he lost track. Dear god, he thought, dear god.

In his old age he developed intricate theories about states of grace. The wife had left him by this point. He thought she lived with the older girl and that they quietly laughed to themselves. Neither was true—the older girl lived alone and laughed loudly to everyone.

The father traced a genealogy of womanly curses on old rolls of fax paper. He asked strangers in the street if they had the mark and demanded to see their palms. He sourced the curses back to biblical times. He came to believe that Elijah had a wife. The last time he saw the younger daughter he wept before her and she called him her son.

LAKE OF EARTH

I

LIGHTS SLIP into the horizon behind him.

The sea lurches. The sky washes his face with cold rain. He wakes. He is handcuffed to an oarless wooden rowboat. Water accumulates in a shallow mirror at the bottom of the vessel.

The droning of waves and rain muddles into static. Half-light tints the air. The sun is hidden somewhere, about to rise.

The man attempts to stand, but the handcuffs restrict him to a hunch. He looks back and views the blank horizon. He turns. Ahead of him grows a brown and green disc: an island.

A tattered shirt hangs wide around his neck. He discovers markings on his shoulder: the word *nemi* in rough script under a crudely drawn bow and arrow.

The sea rages behind him like an engine. He feels the planks groan underneath. The boat approaches the island.

THE BOW BURIES itself into wet sand and chucks the man on his side. He curses and staggers partway up. A beach edged with tall grasses stretches to his left and right. The thick static of waves echoes through his skull. Far away, a dock with several boats tethered to it extends over the water.

His handcuffs are threaded through a metal half-circle bolted to the hull. He pulls against the rusted chain. It snaps—he trips out of the boat and onto the damp beach. The cold tide laps at his clothes.

He stands up and walks inland. Dawn pools sickly over the landscape. The lights of a town shine in the distance. He travels along the steady plain toward them. To his left, the ground rises steeper, then drops off, a clean line separating grass and sky. On the right, in the lowlands, lies a thick forest.

As he walks, his brain attempts connection. He flails at a name for this place, a name for himself, but finds no tether to the concepts. The form of a name exists, but nothing fills the void. He imagines people in general—he sees empty faces, ovals of skin, fingers of indeterminate length. No specific people, only blank structures of flesh.

Further in, the town rises up. He sees an outer ring of uniform two-story buildings. There is no difference between them. He approaches one at random and walks through the open front door.

HE ENTERS a large, quiet room. Occupied beds smother every available surface: unsheeted mattresses, wooden bunks, twin beds on institutional frames, thick cushions layered with blue sheets. In one corner, a table squats beneath food and a bruised tin tank of hot water. The air smells of stacked blankets.

Across the room, two small windows open on the wall of a neighboring building. The muffled light tints the brick in a blue tone that mimics the sea.

He observes the sleeping faces. Some of their mouths unspool lines of spittle, some are clamped shut, others mime speech. Their eyes murmur behind the lids. One woman's mouth gapes. Her chest rises and falls, but she otherwise appears dead.

Fatigue washes over the man. He sees an empty bottom bunk in the far corner of the room.

He lies down and falls asleep.

A LONG BLACK ROAD EXTENDS *and cuts the prairie. He is an old man. He lives in a home encroached upon by nature—the right angle formed by the house and the ground is now a curve. The windows lack glass. Air flows freely in and out.*

The house has no basement, so he digs one. He ferries the dirt in a wheelbarrow and deposits it outside. At night he sleeps in the expanding darkness.

Time passes. He flattens the walls, digs out the corners. He moves his mattress down. Some days he never leaves.

He digs further. He pierces the shovel through some kind of crust. Cold, thick liquid pours through. It rises above his knees. He slips onto his back, floats. The water lifts him. He sleeps until his nose touches the basement ceiling.

His eyes open wide. Two hands emerge from the water. They latch on and pull him under.

THE MAN OPENS his eyes. The underside of a mattress hangs three feet above him. A woman is slouched against the side of his bed. Her hair is a black cloud. She mutters and nods to herself.

The man gets up. Light has forced itself into the room. Even the deepest sleepers are stirring.

A cluster of people mill around the food table, communicating in low voices. The man's hunger is a separate, irate entity inside him. He walks over. The sleepers part and provide the man access to the food. They stare at the split handcuffs around his wrists as he takes a dense puck of bread.

The woman by his bed rushes over. She pulls at his arm. "Listen to me," she says, "Listen."

He pulls away and tries to pour a cup of water, but she grabs his elbow. He twists around to face her and demands to know what she's doing.

She steps back. She clutches her wrists to her sternum and looks through him. "I was young once. I lived alone in a cabin circled by pine trees. I can't tell you how far the forest stretched out. For all I know it went on forever."

The man turns away. She says, "I was born there, I think. One night I looked outside the window and saw two yellow eyes glowing at me. Do you understand what that means? Am I making sense? I could just make out the shape of the beast."

The man swallows his first bite of biscuit. Something in him turns on and his vision staggers. He sees himself as the woman. The thick dough gums in his mouth and he reaches for water. His body is a mutinous thing—all his cells scream in exhaustion and tow him back to bed. He imagines the woman whispering in his ear as he falls asleep. He lifts the cup to his lips and hot water passes between his teeth.

"Over the next few weeks, more of them gathered, always at night, never during the day. They assembled in a ring around the cabin. Something was going to happen. I remember being afraid, but also comforted."

The water tastes like metal, polish, and rot. The man spits it in an arc over the floor. Vomit rises in his throat and he runs. A glorious piercing heat grows at the base of his skull. The woman follows him outside as if tethered.

"Then one of them broke down the cabin door. I ran into the bedroom and they smashed that door too. Just one swipe of the paw. But you know that."

He steps outside into the blinding light.

"You know what it is like to be consumed." She communicates the sensation. He retches into the street.

"They tear you apart, body into pieces. The pain lessens quickly, but I felt all of it. I felt my body separate then reconvene in the beast's stomach. I was dissolved and absorbed. I grew comfortable being part of a whole, diffuse."

He pleads with her to stop.

"A great deal of time passed. I was focused, as if pulled through a lens. I was becoming a new thing. I was sure of this.

"When I first saw the slit of light, I knew I had been born again. I saw my paws and slicked fur. They circled around and held me in their arms. But her, I saw her in the distance. She was tall and bright and entered my vision for only a second."

The man rises and straightens. Their eyes connect. He feels as if two hands, one coming from the woman's eyes, the other from his, are locked. They pass a full minute in this embrace.

He breaks their grasp and hurries toward the center of town. She yells after him, "And then I woke up into this!"

FORWARD. The sleeping houses thin out into smaller, more traditional homes—he sees buildings with space around them, kitchens viewed through open curtains, lawns of low clipped grass. Their front doors are shut; their windows are open.

A high stone wall halts him as he approaches the center of town. People trickle in and out of a raised gate. He passes through.

The inhabitants change. The sleepers, marked by their stumbling gait and slack eyelids, are replaced by citizens that move with purpose and direction. The man feels slapped lucid in their company. He sees shops with open doors, families ambling in and out followed by leashed dogs. Children, he sees children.

Some people turn toward him, then veer away. Some even open their mouths, a gloss of shame obscuring their eyes. He sees black bracelets made of metal on the most distracted. The jewelry has a spike suspended over the skin by rubber connectors.

A woman turns to the man and says, "I was a young boy once. I—" She slaps herself on the wrist and startles backward. She mutters, shakes her head, then shuffles off.

A store the man passes is fronted with a large glass window. He looks in past the display of dried meat and stacked cheese. He sees a worker in a white apron at the counter and two men wearing black suits at a table in the corner.

The sign above the building reads, *No Sleep Food—Deli*. The words are bordered by illustrations of winking pigs in chef's hats.

The sign prods his hunger. He enters.

4

THE FORT BURNS. *The exterior walls—thick tree trunks set in the earth—are swallowed by flames. A black shape escapes past the blinding yellow and white.*

Tapestries, chairs, tables, sawdust, chests, food, straw—it all burns.

The king is old. He cowers in his bedroom. The fire edges toward him. Outside the window is the blank night sky. Below hangs the sea.

The king steps back against the open window frame. He doesn't know the name of the young man who went running, but there was something familiar in his face. The room shakes. He feels himself dissolving, his body like a cavern, eaten away by time and water.

The blaze grasps at his feet. He climbs up and huddles in the window frame. He turns. He stares down at the churning sea.

5

HE WAKES. He remembers going into the deli, a sharp pain, then nothing. Cloth covers his eyes, rope binds his hands. Two fingers jab at the small of his back. He finds himself walking. He hears a pair of voices behind him.

"What happens if she tries to take him?"

"I don't know. A. didn't say."

Silence. Then, "Is it safe here?"

"He wouldn't send us if it weren't safe."

"I remember walking through a forest once. Like this one, but bright green and during the day. Lots of shrubs and vines hanging down from the—"

A smacking noise erupts behind him followed by a cry of pain.

"Ah! Thanks."

"No problem. There was a time I was walking with a man, like this, but I was a young girl. His hands were enormous, and I had—"

He hears another smack and a yelp.

"Thank you."

They keep walking. His ankles are wet and cold, brushed with foliage.

"Do you hear something?"

"No. Wait, I was old once."

The sentence ends with a thud and the shudder of leaves.

"What are you doing? Get up."

Another thud. A second body hits the ground.

He projects his senses—he tries to hear or smell or feel something outside of himself. Wind passes through the leaves. He smells blood and decaying vegetation.

A hand touches his face. The skin is both soft and harsh and somehow he can feel its brightness. The touch, despite his blindfold, allows him to see a wide view—a dark circle of trees and the canopy obscuring the stars. Then closer. He sees two bodies in suits, arrow shafts planted in their backs. The black bracelets hang around their wrists.

He sees himself. Then the hand—he tries to see the hand touching him and the body it possesses, but fails. The body is an absence, a missing frame, a void.

He inhales. He feels the cold air taking residence in his chest. His hunger vanishes. His view widens. He sees the island and the fog surrounding it.

Then the hand withdraws and he is crushed back in his own body. The rope binding his wrists slips off. Five fingers nudge at the small of his back. He walks and the gentle pressure guides him forward. He feels warm breath on his ear.

THE FOREST RECEDES. The pressure at his back vanishes, and he takes it as permission to remove the blindfold. Before him are the last saplings of the forest, then a dirt road blanketed by fog.

A large car putters in his direction. A searchlight mounted to the driver's side door cuts through the mist. It turns and throws all its light on the man, casts him as a shadow. He shields his eyes.

The man hears the car door open and someone yells, "Over here!" A hand waves and obscures the beam of the searchlight.

The man approaches. The passenger door is open. He looks inside. The driver wears a rumpled uniform and cracked leather gloves. His jacket is unbuttoned and a yellowed undershirt hangs loosely around his neck. No black jewelry hangs from his wrists.

The man gets inside.

The car squeals down the road. The driver says, "I'm a representative of a group in town. I promise you're not in any danger." He steers with his knees while he lights a cigarette.

They pass into the outskirts of town. All the houses are dark. The car pulls up to a house just inside the interior wall. The driver gets out and opens the passenger door. "We're here," he says.

6

A NAKED MALE BODY HANGS *unassisted in the air. Someone enters completely swaddled in baggy reams of cloth, pulls a scalpel from one of the folds, and begins to work.*

The swaddled person removes precise cubes of flesh from the body and installs pink tin doors to cover the absences. From the folds of cloth emerge little cloth dolls, less than an inch tall. They are placed on the body. The dolls scurry across the skin and pry open the doors, drop inside. The swaddled person produces props: chairs, tables, beds, umbrellas. These too are placed on the body, and the fabric people snatch them up, drag them into their houses of muscle and skin.

The swaddled person leaves. Time passes. The body opens its eyes. It stands and exits, a low rattle sounding with each step.

7

THE MAN AND THE DRIVER DESCEND creaking stairs into darkness. They enter a basement—the man smells stale air, feels an unfinished dirt floor under his feet.

A bare light bulb turns on. A gray haired man holds the taut brass chain. He wears brown pants and an untucked, filthy dress shirt with the sleeves rolled up. The bulb illuminates dust in the air—it masks the gray haired man's thin face in a filter. Several people stand behind him, their bodies nearly blotted out by darkness.

"Hello," he says. "My name is L." His voice is choked and halting. L. stares into the man's open shirt—the markings on his collarbone are exposed. "This way," he says.

L. walks toward a wooden door in the far wall. They enter a tunnel leading down. Rough planks line the floor and caged bulbs hang from the ceiling. Other tunnels branch off and disappear around curves.

"Your kidnapping was A.'s doing. I want you to know that," L. says.

The man asks what L. does, what is going on here.

"Listen. I was young once. Just an infant, crawling around in the dirt, weaving through their ankles. I remember being scooped up sometimes, held, nursed, then put back down in the dust. They were such extremes—an abundance of intimacy, then a complete lack of it."

L. stops and shakes his head.

"Sorry. Yes. We don't stop our people from dreaming and we don't wear the jewelry. Sometimes I lose focus. She has an inevitable hold on people."

The man asks who she is.

"She is the woman in the forest. She visits the people of the island in their dreams. Then there is A.; he thinks that he is the king. He functions without dreaming, so he oversees everything: food, research, the recovery of objects. He is at war with the woman in the forest."

They reach another wooden door. L. opens it and they step into a rectangular room carved from the earth. At the center a group of men are building a boat. They plane, join, shape. The boat's skeleton rests at the center of the room.

The man begins to ask what they are doing, but L. cuts him off. "The conflict between the woman and A. is useless for both sides. She cannot be killed, and he has so far avoided being deposed."

L. walks over to the frame—he places his hands on the bow and caresses his cheek against the rough wood.

"I was an old man, the captain of a small vessel. It was lovely floating around the sea. I would travel from lighthouse to lighthouse, giving them supplies and pamphlets. Mail too. Sailing up and down the coast. No, that's wrong, not up and down. Just down. The coast had no end."

L. closes his eyes. He smashes his nose into the grain of the wood and inhales deeply.

"Our aim is escape. Except for the few born here, we wash up with no memory of before. The agents we send into the fog outside the island all come back as blank slates."

When he opens his eyes again they are clear.

"Sometimes the fog will lift slightly down by the dock. It might be A.'s efforts weakening her. We plan to wait until it lifts and a crew of strong rowers might make it through."

He stands and makes his way to another door.

"Failure is a constant possibility. Even building the boat challenges us. We might recruit a new builder, but during training he could get lost to the group houses or join A."

They descend into another tunnel.

"I am not the first leader of the movement. I've been the leader multiple times between trips to the sleeping homes. I've spent years there." He shakes his head in quick, nervous jerks.

They enter an egg-shaped cavern twenty feet across. It is half filled with water. Boards hang from the ceiling in a Y and form a path. On the right side a tunnel opens and rises; to the left the planks lead to a sealed metal door.

L. steps over to the door. "I'd like to show you something," he says.

He taps a pattern on the metal door with his knuckles. The door swings open and they step inside.

8

THE LAKE IS *a mirror masked by dust and rippled by time and gravity.*

The lake is underground, reflecting only the cavern roof.

The lake has model ships in it that go in circles. Little men shoot arrows and grappling hooks from ship to ship.

He watches from far away, his view framed by trees. At night he will exit the forest and set the small ships on fire, illuminate the cavern.

He sees a man lounging by the lake in a circular gold mask, his red lips smacking together, bitten raw.

Later. He looks up. The earth ceiling has become transparent. It is a membrane. He can see the sky. He cannot see the sky. He sees dirt again, feels it pressing down, fluid columns of clay and loam dipping into the water. It churns. The sound it makes is the sound of the back of the world being broken.

THE ONLY LIGHT in the room sources from the stub of a candle. A uniformed soldier stands and clumsily salutes L.

An old man, clothed in tatters, sprawls in a chair at the center of the room. His face looks like petrified wood. It registers no changes. His chest doesn't rise or fall, but the man is certain that he is alive.

The man asks who he is.

"One of our agents found him outside the upper woods. There were signs of a struggle—two of A.'s men were found dead around him, shot through with arrows. He was sleeping then, just as he is now. No amount of shaking or noise can wake him.

"It was my predecessor's decision to take him in. He must have lived in the woods, judging by his general filth. We would take him back there if she made some sign of wanting him."

L. bends over and hangs his face in front of the old man's. He grips his worn cheeks, lifts his eyelids and stares at the rolled up white area inside.

"I remember walking through fog. I saw shadows of people on either side. They carried spears and hollered my name. I walked softly. I felt myself getting older and older. My skin wrinkled; my joints dried and cracked. I hobbled across the ground. When she lifted the fog, the searchers no longer recognized me. I was ancient. I was free."

L. lets the old man's eyelids drop. He turns away and rubs his face in his hands. He says, "Some believe the old man will wake when A. is deposed. Then we will supposedly remember our old lives. It's wild speculation, of course—he is a blank slate for our people to put their desires on, and he is therefore useful to us."

L. salutes the guard again. "Come. Let's let the old man rest."

They exit and hear the metal door lock behind them. They take the far tunnel and climb.

On the way up, the man asks why A. is at war with the woman in the forest. L. responds, "He is somewhat mad. There is a pattern she wants him to follow, but he has refused. His son, S., the abomination, is an aspect of his refusal."

L.'s voice grows quiet. "Your tattoo. It marks you as a part of this. I don't fully understand, but I know she brought you here for a purpose."

They climb for some time. The rock walls give way to dirt. L. opens the door in front of them.

A basement, different from the first one. Three men lie face down on the floor. Blood pools around their heads and soaks dark into the dirt. Two giant, gray skinned men hold pipes smeared with red. At the back of the room, a thin man in a suit leans against the wall. "L.," he says. A low grind accompanies his voice.

"What have you done?" asks L.

"They refused us admittance."

"S., you—"

"You should know by now to let us pass. We came for him." S. points at the man.

"You didn't have to kill anyone."

"You gave me no choice. Keep secrets and we will unearth them." S. turns to the gray skinned guards and snaps his fingers. "Put him in the car."

10

THE EMPIRE IS GOOD. *The empire is strong. It takes in two thousand pounds of grain per year. The people are happy. The king is happy.*

The borders are secure. The borders are not expanding. They could expand, but the cost would hurt the empire, and the empire is strong. The empire will keep being strong.

Things will have to go according to plan. The concept of waste has not been factored in. The borders are not expanding. The king is happy; the king is not happy. The sun rises and sets in unnatural intervals that the seers interpret as a sign. They are always interpreting signs. The intestines of crows look the same as they have every year of the empire.

The king spends time tracing shadows on the walls of the keep, the new keep, which is five years old. He avoids hunting in the forest. He only goes there in dreams.

The birth rate has plateaued, but the king swears he sees more and more young men in the palace. He increases security, which only results in more unfamiliar faces, more young men.

The king spends most of the morning dreaming. He wakes up tired and covered in sweat. Some days he wakes screaming, staring at the sun coming in from the balcony.

The empire is good. He sees his life as a fixed line in time and space. The empire is strong. The line stretches in front of him, then stops. He sees an unblemished horizon marking the end.

11

THE GUARDS CROWD around the man in the backseat. A driver wearing a pressed uniform turns onto a road that divides the upper and lower forest.

A lighter clicks and smoke drifts up from the front passenger seat. S. says, "Thank you for coming without struggle." He has thick, cropped hair and wears leather gloves. His sleeve rides up and exposes a perfectly rectangular wrist.

"My father has an offer for you," S. says. "He thinks you can be useful."

The man asks why.

"Often situations don't fall into that kind of logic. Reasons, causes, sources. You can be led to presume ridiculous things from them. Do you understand?"

The man doesn't respond. The forest forms a tunnel of dark green over the road. He looks into the vegetation running by and sees gradients of green, black, and gray—anonymous shapes, forms to project anything into.

"I am one of the few people born on this island. Born, in a sense. What I mean is that I use the word loosely. I understand the island more than most. Do you have a name?"

The man says that he doesn't remember.

"Of course not. You'll have one eventually, one that you choose for yourself. I know this. She describes these rules to me sometimes. Not that I ask for them."

The car exits the forest and speeds toward a cliff-side estate. A cluster of buildings rises above a ten-foot high stucco wall. A whitewashed tower crowned with a ring of glass stretches highest. Two guards flank the entrance and a third slides the gate open.

Groups of people, cleanly dressed and wearing the black jewelry, mill around the open courtyard. The worn cobbles of the driveway are guttered by dust. The car pulls into a row of identical vehicles.

The guards pull him from the car. S. stops them and leans in close to the man. "You should understand, before you meet him, that my father made me. He took others, ones he thought weak, and made me from them."

S. pulls open the collar of his shirt. The man sees inside. He is unsure of the topography of S.'s chest—he knows he sees a jumble of tubes and sinew, bone and what might be coiled wire.

S. holds the man's cheek in his flat, even palm, and says, "Take him up."

THE MAN WATCHES the stairs spiral above, wind in on themselves. He pulls and kicks. The guards redouble their grip and drag him harder.

They arrive at a lacquered red door with a sun cut through it. The guards knock and a muffled, "Come in," sounds from inside.

They enter. An older man, A., sits hunched over a large metal desk cluttered with paper and jumbled components of black jewelry. A beard masks his features. He gestures toward a chair in front of the desk and the guards drop the man into it. A. nods and they leave the room.

A. clears his throat and says, "Tell me what you have learned."

The man pauses and scans A.'s growing smile. The man says that A. is at war.

"That is not entirely accurate—war, at this moment, is too strong a word. I haven't burned down the forest. My people do not go around armed at all times. L. is just hysterical and weak from dreaming." A. drums his fingers on the desk. "I brought you here because I want you to find something for me in the upper forest. It's the seat of her power, a shrine or something—we don't know exactly what form it takes. If you can find it, I'll reward you with a place to live in this compound."

A. pauses and scans the man's face for a sign of a response. He continues, "You need to understand. We aim to eradicate dreaming with these." A. holds up one of the black bracelets. "When the wearer feels an urge to communicate a dream, they slap themselves at the center of the spike. It digs into the skin and distracts them. The bracelets have brought some semblance of order to the island."

The man points out that A. doesn't wear them.

A. laughs. "Not visibly. All my armor is strapped tight around my soul. I have eradicated the dreaming from my body, and I can teach you how to accomplish this. My compound is the best place to learn—she holds little power here."

The man finds his lips and tongue moving. It is as if he encounters the action in himself. "I was an old man once," he says. "I lived by the side of a long road, a highway maybe? In a run down house—"

"Not in here!" A. yells. "Don't invite her in!" He leaps from his chair and across the desk. He slaps the man. Displaced papers spiral and float to the floor.

The man says, "Her hands. She pulled me under." A. hits him again, this time with a balled fist. The man's nose spurts. A line of blood extends down his face.

A. bellows, "Do you understand what she does? She takes away our voice, our power to choose for ourselves. You must learn control!" A. circles the man. "You see her rotting power, don't you? The dreams remove you from the world, the real world, the one in which you are flesh and blood. Your visions are only the garble made by your idle brain. But she sanctifies and empowers them."

The man watches A.'s chest heave. He wipes sweat from his eyes. His actions are separate and distinct—thumb wiping above the brow, mouth open, then closed. There exists an element of performance to it. He walks around the desk and falls into his chair.

The man says that there are moments when he dreams wide awake. He says that they are just flashes of things: burning buildings, an old man leaping into the sea, a forest, guards with faces he doesn't recognize.

A. replies, "They are false symbols. She wants you to believe that you are fated, doomed, but there is choice in all things." He grins as if remembering something. "Let me show you the library."

THEY CLIMB the tower stairs, the man first, then A. The man halts. He grows nauseous. Short bursts of images struggle to break through a barrier in his brain: the moon sinking into the sea, a man falling through the air trailed by a ribbon of blood, a tree bent to the ground, an old man muttering curses, and her—he thinks he saw her for just a second.

A. puts his hand on the man's shoulder and the images stop. His stomach rights itself. They continue up the stairs.

THE WALLS OF THE round tower library are smothered in bookshelves. Around the room are four metal tables covered with sheets of paper. A robed man, its only occupant, reassembles pages with tweezers and a magnifying glass. He nods to A., moves a scrap of paper a quarter turn, then exits.

The man investigates the shelves. He finds a few complete books, the spines blooming with aged glue and linen. Most are just loose pages in labeled plastic bags.

"All things that come to the island wash up on the beaches. Water damage has claimed most of them. A well sealed trunk or suitcase occasionally arrives with some damp paperbacks inside, but the bulk of these we must reassemble. We usually find just a few pages at a time. The initiate who was in here puts them together as best he can."

The man looks down at one of the tables. In the center, surrounded by a radius of documents, lies a grayed piece of paper. It looks newly assembled—a lace of drying glue shines on its surface.

It reads:

—is overlooked by the Town of Nemi, some twenty miles north of Rome. The lake sits at the crater of a long extinct volcano and possesses an even, circular shape.

Many sunken Roman ships were found there—a nearby museum houses relics from the latest excavation. Highlights include preserved——of wine, sets of——and weaponry,—a bronze—of—

The center of the page fades into illegibility, but becomes clearer near the end:

—woods—pre-Grecian cult———. The— Nemorensis was challenged —, ——fought with branches until—was—— victor. They were escaped slaves———granted asylum by the cult. No temple stands by the lake—the only mark of the Nemorensis's power was an open-air fane.

The man asks why A. doesn't just try and escape the island.

"Like L.? No, we've tried—she has fully closed that avenue. Our only escape will be when she is dead."

The man mentions the lights on the horizon.

"Yes, the lifting fog. It could be part of her trickery. She could be luring us out to crush our boats on some hidden reef."

The man looks at the page. He stares at the circle in the center. He asks him what will happen if he tries to leave the compound.

"You'll be required to stay until you decide to help us. You are too dangerous to let wander."

A. pauses for a second, runs a finger along his lips. "Let me put it another way. I don't believe in fate; it is an absurd concept meant to rationalize events we fail to predict. But look at the choices in your brief life. Look back. See the line they have made, the direction they take you. You see the forest, don't you? Close your eyes; picture it. You see a line taking you there."

The man closes his eyes. He sees his life so far as a line. He cannot imagine any other possibilities. The future remains blank. He cannot see the forest. He only pictures the island from above, a circle floating in the boiling sea.

A BLACK CAR SQUEALS AWAY. The man stands at the blurred edge of the upper forest. The white disc of the moon hovers just above the highest branches. He walks in.

The man draws a map in his head. He marks particular features—a cracked limb bowing into the ground, a bird's nest in forked branches, the crease of an old trail—but these blend and repeat, as if he is going in circles or being mocked by the terrain. He then chooses to walk blindly, forget the map. He travels further in.

The trees crowd together, thin and compact. He slides sideways between them. The light shrinks. Ahead stands a circular wall of saplings. The man pries himself an opening and forces through to the other side.

Three feet of soft, short grass, then the tree. Branches sprout from every surface. They begin at the ground and spiral up its looping structure. The whole thing is like an enormous bud—it carries the potential to burst open at any moment. A skin of heavy bark peers out from between the branches.

The man discovers a slight mound just before the base of the tree. A gun rests on it. He cradles it, tests its weight in his hands.

He looks up at the tree. Wind whips through the manifold of leaves. The whole thing shakes like a human form. The rustling branches rise into a choir.

The man grows tired. He lies down on the soft grass in front of the tree. He clutches the gun close and falls asleep.

1 2

TWO MONKS—*one old, one young—crest the ridge and look into the valley below. They see a village down there.*

The community is small and little-known. The inhabitants were converted by traveling clergy a decade ago. A wooden cross rises on one side of the church. The parish minister that sent for them vanished days before their arrival.

The men have no record of the town's faith before the conversion.

The minister sent them reports of a monstrous fox in the area. An infant was stolen from its crib, smudged blood found on the stone floor.

Lambs were slaughtered outside their fences—their shepherd discovered the remains on the last snows of early spring.

Only two villagers have actually seen the fox. They reference its large size and hunched back. It resembles nothing they have ever witnessed. But it is a fox, they are sure.

The monks see the fox as a penance. The old man explains: there is a time before people are aware of their sins, but this period is still judged. We must fight the demon and show our worthiness. God tests us, he says.

They gather provisions and two crossbows. The men leave town, follow the animal's winding tracks into the foothills.

AT NIGHT THE FOX COMES and talks to the young monk. It whispers in his ear as he falls asleep. It tells him about the time before. It explains that the child was murdered and thrown down a well. The lambs were killed by a disturbed adolescent.

I have been forsaken, the fox whispers.

The young man views the fox not as a hulking beast but a sleek, red blur seen only in motion.

THE OLD MONK GROWS thinner on their rations. He laughs as he ties his robe tighter and tighter. Days pass; his gray hair knots.

The young man tracks the path of the sun through the sky and is sure that they are lost. He sees messages and patterns in the budding branches. He reflects on forces and signs. The tracks of the fox are looping, incongruous things. When the young man tries to hold their path in his head his vision blurs.

THE OLD MAN WHISPERS: *See, there it is. The fox sleeps twenty yards away on a moss-covered rock. The creature's openness shocks the young man. It should be in a nest or a shell, a corner or a burrow.*

The old man raises his crossbow and tells his companion to do the same. The young man closes one eye. The red dot of the fox notches into the sight at the end of the weapon.

The young man hears voices, hundreds of them. He turns and brings the end of his weapon into contact with the old man's temple. The voices fall silent, revealing a background noise like water running over glass. The old monk turns. His mouth is a wide O.

THE YOUNG MAN WALKS *into town in robes soaked red. The inhabitants watch. He lacks his backpack and weapon. He appears as if transformed into an earlier version of himself.*

He approaches the church. The cross hanging outside is rough and old, as if made from driftwood. The young man passes through the threshold. The pews are empty and covered in dust. Debris skitters across the floor. Light rains in though a pattern of holes in the roof. This is a long abandoned place.

The fire rises and lasts all through the night.

13

HE WALKS back toward town. He plans to go to the cafe and wait in the corner for someone to retrieve him. He sees himself motionless in a chair, back against the wall. His thoughts are still-frames.

At the outskirts, a black car squeals sideways in front of him. The day breaks. S. and two guards jump out of the car.

S. says, "You should have come back to the estate."

The man draws the gun, levels it at the first guard and pulls the trigger. He shifts his aim to the right. He pulls the trigger again. Two red clouds hang in the air. The bodies lie motionless on the ground.

Inside his mind there is a plan that extends up to a point and disappears. If it continues past that point, it is invisible. No trace of his mind is bothered by this.

The driver exits the vehicle and runs toward the estate. The man grabs S. and shoves him in the backseat. S. struggles and the man brings the butt of the gun down into the side of his head.

The man climbs into the driver's side. Sleepers, awakened by the gunfire, stumble from the homes. He drives further into town.

THE MAN PULLS S. down the basement stairs. He has tied his wrists together and attached a short tether. Blood soaks through S.'s blindfold and streaks down his face.

The basement is empty. In the far corner, four of L.'s men lie on the ground, their heads spilled out on the dirt floor. The door at the far end of the room is hacked to pieces.

The man and S. descend. They hear footsteps running through adjacent tunnels, screams permeating the layers of dirt and rock.

They reach the egg-shaped chamber. The old man's guard lies face down in the dark water. The metal door hangs from one hinge. The cavern smells like smoke and ash.

They enter the old man's room. His body sprawls, his chair knocked over and broken, his eyes gouged out. Blood haloes around his head; red-brown footprints form a corona around the body. Precise squares of skin are cut from his neck and his right arm ends at the elbow.

The man sees an open book on the floor. A section is highlighted:

Where is she? I went back and the lake was deserted, dry. The bones of sunken ships stuck out of the lakebed. The sky was red and wet and the forest burned all around me.

On the way back up, the man sees no sign of L.

A CHAIN OF SMALL ISLANDS SHRINKS *until the emerging rocks are drowned. The king is an old man. Tatters hang from his frame. There is someone behind him wearing an iron helmet and holding a long branch like a sword.*

The king's hands are blistered and raw. Wounds and sores dance up his arms. The sun is immersed in the southern waters. He scrambles along the little islands. His mind feels like a sponge, thoughts washing in and out like tides.

An idea creeps in. He looks at the horizon and sees the white lines of waves, then the lights. Some scraps of memory float in. Hands, feet, elbows, toes: no complete bodies, just parts. He looks behind him, then in front. He is running out of unsubmerged rocks. He breathes deep.

Cool water laps at his bare feet. He looks backward, forward.

There was a life before this, he thinks. There is a life after.

PAST THE BLUFFS, the sea extends out to meet the horizon. S. and the man sit among the tall grasses as the wind coming off the water whips around them. Behind them is a thirty-foot cliff; it drops down to the beach. The man points the gun at S. and time passes like this.

A car approaches. It leaves the road and rattles across the choppy ground toward them.

The man stands and pulls S. up. He clutches the back of S.'s neck and presses the barrel into his temple. A. and two guards get out of the car.

A. yells, "What are you doing? What is the meaning of this?"

The man backs up as A. approaches. "I'll shoot him if you come any further. I'll throw him over the cliff."

A. stops and raises his hands, palms out. He says, "My son never hurt you."

"You will both leave the island. You will go immediately down to the docks and take a boat away from here."

"You want control over these people? What do you hope to gain from this? Power? Wealth?"

The man digs the gun harder into S.'s head. "You have been here far too long. I've seen the visions. How many have come for you?"

A.'s shoulders drop. His eyes darken. "I've drowned them all."

"Go to the docks. When—"

"I will drown you with them," A. says. "Go to the beach at the upper shore; look under the waves. When I am dead, my son will rule."

"That's not going to happen."

"What privilege does she have? When I tear down the shrine, when I lay her body out in the middle of town, then—"

The wind coming off the sea crescendos and consumes A.'s words. The man says, "We have the same dreams. You know this. You've seen the fox, haven't you?"

A.'s hands grip tightly, curl in on themselves. "Give me my son back."

"Only at the docks. I'll let you leave."

"No. She won't allow it."

"I won't make you walk into—"

S. twists around and bites deep into the man's wrist. Blood spurts and clouds his square, white teeth. The man screams and lurches back. His foot hovers over empty space.

A. runs forward. He extends his arm. His fingers spread wide. The man and S., wrapped together, a bundle, tip backward. A flash of light. A gunshot. A hand, a tuft of hair, and a streak of red peer over the edge of the cliff.

The man's mind is empty as he passes through the air. The visions inhabit his body without any discussion or conflict. They bury themselves in his flesh.

A BLACK MARK IN THE SAND. It moves. S. lies underneath the man, a neat red hole burrowed in his chest, his left forearm a jumble of metal and loose skin. Yellow and red fluid trickles down the sand toward the sea. The man stands.

The tide edges up the coast. A. runs to the man, his chest heaving, his coat flapping behind him.

The man sees the dropped gun embedded in the sand. He dives, grabs it, aims. He shoots one round in front of A. and sand bursts at his feet. A. stops. They stand twenty feet apart.

A. holds his hands above his head. His chest heaves. He looks at S.'s body as if through layers of fog. "He was so beautiful. I remember cutting apart the layers of vellum and pulling him dripping and screaming from the vessel. His arms were structureless things. I wish I could see that, see it as he did."

A. pauses and closes his eyes. "I want another life. I would like to be stripped of myself. I want to be born as something new and clean and beautiful. But all I see now is a line."

He yells above the wind, "I was old, floating in a featureless ocean. The sky was clouded the color of the water and the waves rose and the waves fell. I felt their patterns of movement, the moon pushing and pulling at my back. The horizon is clean and empty!"

The man sees little homes, towns and cities collapsing inside A.

"Have you had this dream?" he asks. "Do you see it? Or is it in front of you, somewhere in the distance?"

The guards run down the beach toward them, thirty feet away now.

A. swallows and closes his eyes. "Is there—"

The man shoots him twice in the chest. A. collapses into the wet sand.

The man walks over to the body. A wheezing sound escapes from A.'s chest. His eyes glaze over and he is gone.

The guards approach the body. They watch his eyes close. The tide pushes silt into his hair. The guards leave.

Behind a thick mass of gray clouds, the sun goes down. The beach is obscured by blue and purple darkness. The man drops the gun. He stares at the blank horizon. The color of sea and sky merge. All he sees is a dome over him, a sphere, a cage.

TIME PASSES. The town changes. The large group houses multiply and take root even at the center of town.

The road between the upper and lower forest succumbs. Only a small footpath remains—it errs off the former route and leaves travelers wandering in circles. In the deepest parts of the forest, no light passes through the canopy, but the vegetation glows as if from within.

The man lives alone in A.'s former estate. Vines crumble the plaster. The sea on one side erodes the cliff. The outer wall has already tumbled into the water.

He finds a home in the basement, a single room with an airshaft that ekes in a bit of light. He has no hunger there. He has a bed of straw and the gun. He feels a name perched on the edge of his lips. He carves the same map into the wall over and over. He pictures the island from above as a solid disc of green.

In his visions, the man sees new people coming to the island, washing ashore, an exodus. He dreams he is a young woman with a gold moon in her hair. He dreams that something chases her, something he is too terrified to look back and see. Some days he never wakes.

The upper shore changes. The tide drops and bare stone islands emerge from the coast. They lead into open water. The man sees them in his head like a prophecy.

At the tip, at the last island. Lights on the horizon. There is another world outside of this one. There is a life after this.

THE LAKE,
THE OTHER LAKE,
AND ALL THE BLOOD
GONE OUT OF HIM

THE WATER PASSES long and wide. I float and watch the pillars of earth that have risen from the lakebed. They tower thirty feet high, five feet wide, rimmed by moats of erosion. The dirty water sifts through my toes as I kick. The lake is never deeper than I am tall, and I am very tall.

I hear them whisper, catch them watching: the children, ragged and filthy, blotting out the sun as they leap from pillar to pillar above me.

The water drifts me to the steep banks. Overhanging trees filter light coming from the sky ribboned with clouds. The water grows quiet and cold beneath the branches.

I find a corner where the lake ends. A trail lifts from the shallows and the forest opens around it. I haul myself dripping from the water. I walk forward down the path.

THE TRAIL ENDS at another lake. Here everything shines green and blue, glimmered and battered by light. At my step, the wet clay pushes back firm and slick, almost ceramic. My skin contracts against the cold water.

The filthy children have followed me in and come close. They whisper a story in my ear. They tell me about a boy of their group who grew too large. They say, see the stain by the edge of the water? He was empty when we threw him in.

At the center of the lake the water grows gray and drops out like a tunnel. The path behind me has vanished. The children crowd around and push me toward the shore. I swing my fists and pummel a few, but they get a good grip and drag me to the waterline. I ask them if there is a third lake and the few not pulling roll and roll with laughter.

I scream and scream. I hear them roar until I am empty, under, and gone.

CHARACTERISTICS
OF ABERRATIONAL
CULTIC MOVEMENTS

1

THE HOUSE, THE HOUSE. It sits by a river outside of town, flanked by unkempt fields. We describe it to potential recruits as pastoral, Edenic. It stands three stories tall, houses seventeen people. It used to be open, now it is shut.

2

MARTIN ONCE WORKED in ad sales at the local newspaper. He left and arrived at places promptly. The child, his child, hung around his heels at all times.

This was before he put his hand under scalding water and saw steam rising from his fingers. He couldn't tell if the steam sourced from the water or his hand. The burning sensation came later, but he failed to locate the cause of the pain.

He came to describe it as rapture.

Then the shedding of the wife and child, the deadlocked door of the house, the knocking of concerned neighbors and friends.

He emerged three weeks later, burns parading up his arms, carrying three books: The Book of Light, The Book of the World, and one with no title which none of us have read.

3

AFTER WE ARE DEEMED trustworthy, Martin shows us The Book of Light. It details the true nature of light—how it acts and smells and affects things in the world.

He explains how light will become deadly, like rain changing to hail. One splashes, the other pummels until the body is pliant.

The light, he yells. Martin splays his fingers against the giant window in the living room and screams about the immanently perforated masses. The sun blankets him.

We tell our families. We implore them to come down to the house by the river. There is more than enough room.

4

THE BOOK OF THE WORLD contains a random inventory of objects. It documents the state of all things before The Book of Light, sometimes in specific terms, more often in general. Mildew damaged shirts, plaster molds of hands, Bell jars of fused toffees. Halves of guns. Few of us have made it through the Book.

5

SOMEONE HAS TO SEAL up the house when the bad light arrives. Martin asks for a volunteer, and a thin white hand shakes up. His name is Timothy and he has no family. We took him a year and four months ago from the streets of town.

He is sent to martyrdom at noon of the next day. The entrance hall clutters with boards, duct tape, nails, a tall ladder, and Timothy. He steps outside and quickly closes the doors to contain the increasingly toxic light. Martin himself nails the entryway shut from the inside. We huddle in the basement, listening to the pounding from upstairs. It is well into the night before it stops.

When we come up from the basement, all the windows are boarded over. All avenues of light are taped, sealed, contained.

We know the sun is rising when we hear the screaming. We listen to his proclamations about boiling skin and fires tearing through the sky. There are people coming toward him, he says. Martin holds us back from the sealed door.

Time passes. The screaming stops.

We remember him asleep on the couch, shirtless, tucked in a sleeping bag. We saw his white, freckled chest recede and contract, patchy chest hair rustling against the flannel lining.

6

WE LIVE on the first floor with our father, a tall, lumbering man. His hands nearly scrape the ground when he walks.

We have free rein of the house. There are no other children, so people get a far off look in their eyes when they see us and pay no attention. They don't lock their doors or drawers. Everything is open to us.

We have memories of before. Of the mother and the light. They are fuzzy and indistinct, but the smells pierce through. We used to press our noses to the lawn and inhale the grass, let it poke all the way up our nostrils. We do this sometimes on the basement floor, but the earth there smells like turpentine and urine.

7

THE BASEMENT: one large main area, two smaller rooms with blue plastic tarps stretched out over the floors.

Laura lives in a corner room. She says her bones used to be full of disease, but now they are clean and hollow, like a bird's. Her possessions—a stack of books, boxes of clothes, a lamp, a bedside table—keep down the corners and prevent the plastic from sliding. She sleeps on a quilted twin mattress.

8

DAVIS LIVES on the first floor, in the pantry. He sleeps swaddled in a pea green blanket surrounded by cans and old, yellowed cookbooks. He tells us that the first thing he sees in the morning is the large silver stockpot on the floor.

He was a pizza boy. He had little to contribute; that's why he sleeps in the pantry.

9

THE RITUALS TAKE PLACE in the master bedroom. We observe through a keyhole.

Christine—we think her name is Christine—stands in front of Martin and takes her clothes off. We see her shoulder blades rise and fall, pinched Vs in her back. She lies down on the bed, out of our line of view. We only see her naked feet. Her toes are long; we wonder how and if our toes will ever get that long.

He takes an old paint can and dips a thick, frayed brush. The brush disappears from view. Then sounds, like splashing. We see him run the brush over her feet and cover them with a thin gloss.

She makes a sound like sand flowing. He pulls out a wet, dripping rope that seems to source from her head.

Once a week, different people, all women.

10

LEO ARCHER SWEARS there were only three rooms on the second floor. Now there are four, that fact is indisputable.

We make maps on lined paper. When it changes again, we will know.

11

OUR MOTHER WOULDN'T COME. She stood outside our apartment door and smashed her white fists against the wood while we snuck out the fire escape.

We clutched blankets and clothes, our father laden with two suitcases and a thickly strapped backpack.

12

THE LARDER IS half full. When Davis wakes, he sees more and more white paint on the walls of the pantry. The fresh fruit is long gone; the remnants pile in the basement trash pit.

Soap. We try and make soap but lack several crucial ingredients. The results come to a thick gray liquid that makes things neither clean nor dirty.

Martin spends more time in the bedroom. We hear the sound of paper endlessly turning over, the whack of slamming books.

No sound comes from the outside world. No screams, no knocks, no whispers.

13

THE DOOR TO THE ATTIC IS boarded over, but we find a duct in the third floor walls. We sneak up during house meetings.

The roof is ramshackle and shot through with shafts of light. Timothy must have been unable to cover it. We take great care to duck under the bright beams when we travel to the attic's center.

There is a spot where we can sit and be surrounded by a cage of blinding angles. The wood underneath feels hot and rough. It touches back. The air reeks of insulation. When we lie on our sides we hear the sounds of the house underneath like a creaking mattress.

There are some days we don't miss the old world at all.

14

ELI PUTS his hands on all of us but never says why.

15

A SECOND FLOOR BEDROOM DOOR IS barred from the inside. Some people remember a woman named Robin living in the room, but Eli claims it was a man named Leo, who pipes up and says that he is still there. Either way, reports are sketchy. Jeff slams his shoulder into the door, but it doesn't give way.

Some claim the room is absent from physical reality, and the locked door prevents us from being swallowed into nothingness. Others claim that Robin or Leo (Leo again proclaims his existence) smashed their way to the outside world as an act of suicide or escape. Perhaps something broke through from the outside. The locked, barred door is intended to save us.

We fall asleep imagining a jagged hole in the wall. It opens into bare, toxic light.

16

MARTIN EMERGES, glossy, from his room. Gather in the living room, he says. We move the sleeping bags and general clutter—paper, plastic forks, dust, fully-leafed magazines—to the corners of the room. He claims he is ready to show us the third book.

The writing is sketchy and lacks the directness of the preceding works. It includes illustrations of basic interactions like hugging, holding hands, slapping, but with distance between the contact. He explains that the concepts of cause and effect will break down. We will raise our hand in anger and somewhere a faucet will turn on. We will move to embrace one another and find ourselves covered in dust. Our footsteps will be rain.

17

WE EAT salads of kidney beans and baby corn. They have either no dressing or a dusting of flour which merges everything into a paste.

Our joints are angry and rusted. We see ourselves as failing machines. Jeff pours over The Book of the World. When we ask him what he is looking for he has no concrete answer.

We ask Martin pointed questions about God. He responds by directing us to obscure passages that supposedly prove there is no God, that we confuse God with the system we are in, the closed loop. He says that if we stay in the house, we can make it through to the other side and live the new world in its infancy.

He uses images of rebirth. Spring. The best things we imagine these days are bright green.

18

YELLING PIERCES the floor. Footsteps, then the sound of something metal being gouged into wood.

A splintering, a crashing to the floor. Someone saw.

There are some days we see the old world as clearly as ever, as if through the act of remembering we can bring it back.

They climb the narrow stairs to the attic and see us in the center, surrounded by a cage of light. Our father is there, waving his arms and yelling. He gets right up to the light but won't enter. Martin's mouth is wide open. We hear the words, careful, dear god, careful. Come toward us, they say.

We imagine methods to bring the old world back. If we are to understand that effects do not match their causes, then there must be some inscrutable action that restores the world to it's previous state.

This has led us to catalogue and attempt all available options. We have knelt on all stairs. We have filled all shoes with every source of water. We have flooded the rooms with smoke. All actions are exhausted except for one.

We stand.

We step forward.

We twist our faces upward into the light.

THIS IS HOW WE
MOVE THROUGH HOMES

1

I WAS BORN into the forest with a memory of searching. My palms hung white, marked by cold rain sluicing through the canopy.

An abandoned house rose from the green floor. Plants grew into it, a reclamation effort. I climbed the collapsed porch, entered.

2

WHAT I KNOW:

The homes are all abandoned.

They exist in varying stages of decay.

Evidence of habitation, then evacuation, litters them.

3

A TWO-STORY BRICK HOUSE with a collapsed chimney. Objects: a violin, a Boston bicentennial commemorative silver plate, TV trays, three yellow ribbons in a glass box, a shotgun barrel clogged with soil, sheet metal, and a white circle where a clock hung.

4

THE COMMON, puncturing memory of a gate: metal scraping on metal, the bottom right corner digging into dirt, a sharp creak. They are thinly connected, as if by long, loose strands of thread.

The last memory is of it unceasingly open, soundless.

5

PLACE A BLACK STONE, irregular but smooth, into a wide, clear wall. Some transformation occurs. The wall is made soft and permeable, like an inch thick layer of wet clay.

Movement can then take place.

I close my eyes and pass through. When I open them the stone has fallen to the floor, the wall is solid, and I am in a new home.

6

A BLUE THREE-STORY HOUSE. The yard is seeded with shingles. Objects: a drawer of rings, four small bells, three rolls of yellow toilet paper stacked under the sink, a tooth, a can of red spray paint, seven black garbage bags burst by expanding wet leaves, two bibles, and a box of gray matches.

7

THE CEILING OF LEAVES, the black-blue spots of sky, the stars. Wind stirs the canopy. I recognize common shapes: branches, leaves, moss. Then that recognition exits. The canopy is a net, a screen, a ceiling caved in.

8

THIS HOME RESEMBLES the others, but new in all available ways. I am not sure how I arrived or departed.

Nothing is abandoned; all things here have people to claim them.

THE BODY IS a white silhouette on the ground. I stare at it for hours before realizing what it is.

It is small and light, almost hollow. I remember the act of carrying and the travel of crunching leaves.

THIS HOUSE IS FILLED with the presence of another. I think to call out and welcome him, but halt at the memory of chasing.

I find the man, a dark shape, leaning over a sputtering faucet, washing something off his hands. My footsteps make no sound.

SOMEWHERE IN THE WOODS I find the open gate. I place her body inside, laid out on the gravel path between rectangles of lawn.

I close the gate behind me. The sound connects and forms with scraping metal. All things here have people to claim them.

THERE ARE OTHERS, I am sure. I have found their notes, their footsteps in dust, their hair and flakes of skin. I have found their new, recent traces of decay.

I am certain I am not going around in circles.

I am certain that I will someday turn a corner or pass through a wall and someone will be there to greet me.

ACKNOWLEDGMENTS

Many thanks to the editors of the journals in which these stories first appeared: *Elimae* ("Treatment" and an excerpt from "Lake of Earth"), *Gigantic Sequins* ("Five Cites"), *Caketrain* ("Characteristics of Aberrational Cultic Movements"), and *Lies/Isle* ("This Is How We Move Through Homes").

This book would not have been possible without the support of my parents, John and Janene, and my sisters, Maggie and Rain.

Thanks to my professors at Metropolitan State University of Denver, in particular Rebecca Gorman, Theresa Crater, and Elsie Haley.

Thanks to Amanda Raczkowski and Joseph Reed for your precision and care in bringing this book to life.

Above all, this book is for Lauren.

ABOUT THE AUTHOR

William VanDenBerg lives with his wife in Denver. He can be found online at williamvandenbergwrites.com.

CPSIA information can be obtained at www.ICGtesting.com
Printed in the USA
BVOW03s1541061113

335337BV00001B/2/P